BEAR FOR BREAKFAST

Robert Munsch

Illustrated by
Jay Odjick

North Winds Press
An Imprint of Scholastic Canada Ltd.

The artwork for this book was drawn digitally on a tablet monitor.

The type is set in Constantia.

Library and Archives Canada Cataloguing in Publication

Munsch, Robert N., 1945-, author
Bear for breakfast / by Robert Munsch ; illustrated
by Jay Odjick.

ISBN 978-1-4431-7054-3 (hardcover)

I. Odjick, Jay, illustrator II. Title.

PS8576.U575B43 2019   jC813'.54   C2018-904819-0

www.scholastic.ca

Photos ©: back cover background: Volykievgenii/Dreamstime.

6 5 4 3 2 1   Printed in Canada 114   19 20 21 22 23

MIX
Paper from
responsible sources
FSC
www.fsc.org   FSC® C016245

To Donovan Montgard,
La Loche, Saskatchewan.
— R.M.

For Mom
— J.O.

Donovan and his grandfather looked in the refrigerator.

"There is nothing to eat," said Donovan. "Absolutely nothing to eat."

"There is lots of stuff!" said his mother. "I just went shopping."

"I want bear for breakfast," said Donovan. "Grandpa told me that he used to eat bear!"

"Well, the grocery store does not have bear," said Donovan's mom. "How about some cereal?"

"I'll go get a bear," said Donovan.

"Right," said his mom. "If you catch one fast, we can still have it for breakfast."

So Donovan walked down the street looking for a bear.

His feet went *thump, thump, thump, thump, thump* and he yelled, "Bear, bear, bear, bear, bear!"

Behind him he heard something going *trip, trip, trip, trip, trip* and saying in a very high voice, "Kid, kid, kid, kid, kid!"

He turned around and saw an ant.

Donovan yelled, "Go away, ant!"

The ant said, *"Aaaaaaaaaahhhhhh!"* and ran away.

Donovan kept on walking down the street. His feet went *thump, thump, thump, thump, thump* and he yelled, "Bear, bear, bear, bear, bear!"

After a while he heard something behind him making noises like this: *trip, trip, trip, trip, trip* and saying in a high voice, "Kid, kid, kid, kid, kid!"

He turned around and saw a squirrel.

Donovan yelled, "Go away, squirrel!"

The squirrel said, *"Aaaaaaaaahhhhhh!"* and ran away.

Donovan kept walking down the street. His feet went *thump, thump, thump, thump, thump* and he yelled, "Bear, bear, bear, bear, bear!"

After a while he heard something walking behind him. It sounded like this: *trap, trap, trap, trap, trap.*

He turned around and saw a dog.

Donovan yelled, "Go away, dog!"

The dog said, *"Aaaaaaahhhhhh!"* and ran away.

So Donovan went into the woods. His feet went *thump, thump, thump, thump, thump* and he kept yelling, "Bear, bear, bear, bear, bear!"

After a while he heard something behind him going *BLAM, BLAM, BLAM, BLAM, BLAM* and saying in a deep voice, **"KID, KID, KID, KID, KID."**

Donovan turned around and there was an enormous bear, big like a school bus.

Donovan looked at it and said, "I'm not scared of you, bear."

The bear opened its big mouth and growled at Donovan: *"Grrrrrrrrrrrr!"*

Donovan said, "Time to go, time to go!" He tiptoed away: *TIP, TIP, TIP, TIP, TIP.*

And the bear went *TIP, TIP, TIP, TIP, TIP* after him.

"Aaaaaaahhhhhh!" yelled Donovan, and he started to walk: *PAT, PAT, PAT, PAT, PAT.*

And the bear went *PAT, PAT, PAT, PAT, PAT* after him.

"Aaaaaaahhhhhh!" yelled
Donovan. He started to run:
*WHOMP, WHOMP, WHOMP,
WHOMP, WHOMP.*

And the bear ran after him:
*WHOMP, WHOMP, WHOMP,
WHOMP, WHOMP.*

Donovan ran all the way
home and slammed the door.

"Yo, Donovan!" said his mom.
"Where is your bear?"
"Coming right now!" yelled Donovan,
and the bear crashed through the
kitchen door.

Donovan's mom said, "Time to go, time to go!" She tiptoed around the kitchen table: *TIP, TIP, TIP, TIP, TIP.*

And the bear went *TIP, TIP, TIP, TIP, TIP* after her.

"*Aaaaaahhhhh!*" yelled Donovan's mom. She started to walk around the kitchen table: *PAT, PAT, PAT, PAT, PAT.*

And the bear went after her: *PAT, PAT, PAT, PAT, PAT.*

"Aaaaaaahhhhhh!" yelled
Donovan's mom, and she started
to run around the kitchen table:
*WHOMP, WHOMP, WHOMP,
WHOMP, WHOMP.*
And the bear ran after her:
*WHOMP, WHOMP, WHOMP,
WHOMP, WHOMP.*

Just as the bear was going to catch her, Donovan's grandfather hit it on the head with a frying pan: *BONNNGGG!*

The bear yelled, "*OUCH!*" and went out the door. Donovan's grandfather said, "There goes breakfast!"

"Pizza," said Donovan, "does not have big teeth. Let's have pizza for breakfast."